To Sarah
From Mommy & Daddy, Christmas 1976

CAT O' NINE TALES

AS TOLD TO
LOUIS UNTERMEYER

Illustrated by Lawrence Di Fiori

AMERICAN HERITAGE PRESS   NEW YORK

Published by American Heritage Press, a subsidiary of McGraw-Hill, Inc.
Published in Canada by McGraw-Hill Company of Canada, Ltd.
Library of Congress Catalog Card Number: 70-149736
07-065937-0 (trade); 07-065938-9 (library)
2 3 4 5 6 7 8 9 0 HDBP 7 5 4 3 2

For KAT
sometimes known as
Kathleen N. Daly

CONTENTS

A Foreword _____ 7

The First Life
HOW I BECAME A GOD _____ 9

The Second Life
HOW I SAVED MY COUNTRY _____ 17

The Third Life
HOW I LED AN ARMY _____ 27

The Fourth Life
HOW I BECAME HUMAN _____ 32

The Fifth Life
HOW I MADE FRIENDS WITH MICE _____ 41

The Sixth Life
HOW I CREATED A KING _____ 49

The Seventh Life
HOW I RODE ON A BROOMSTICK _____ 60

The Eighth Life
HOW I MADE A POOR BOY RICH _____ 78

The Ninth Life
HOW I CAME TO LIFE FOR AN HOUR _____ 90

One More Word _____ 95

A FOREWORD

It is said that a cat has nine lives. I know that *I* have—or have had. What's more, I remember every single one of them. I've told stories about each of them so often that I am called the Cat o' Nine Tales. It's a kind of joke, for the original cat-o'-nine-tails was a whip, a whip with nine knotted tails used for striking. I suppose you could say that my tales also are striking, but they never hurt anyone.

How do I remember them? I might say they remember me. They come back to me in dreams. After I've had dinner—sometimes it's leftovers, sometimes it's liver, sometimes (when I'm lucky) it's kidneys and cream—I lie in front of the fireplace. I wash myself all over, lazily, luxuriously. Warm and content in the best of all possible worlds, I drowse. My eyes close and my mind opens.

Then the dreams begin. There are nine of them, nine lives. They take me everywhere, from time to time, from place to place. I change with them. I become a different cat and live an entirely different kind of life in every different kind of country.

My first life goes back four thousand years. It started in a marshy jungle. . . .

THE FIRST LIFE
HOW I
BECAME
A GOD

My first life goes back four thousand years. It started in a marshy jungle. The trees were so thick they almost shut out the sun. But it was warm, wet and warm, and busy with birds. Plovers and partridges chased each other; the great river that rushed by was alive with cranes and flamingos, herons, kingfishers, and all sorts of bright-colored ducks. There were bats—thousands of them—lizards, and scorpions, but not many other animals. Once in a while, a lion wandered in among the reeds and tall grasses, but he did not stay; he was at home only in rocky places and on the sandy plains of the desert. There was plenty of food; the river swarmed with fish, and I could have all I wanted with a few scoops of the paw.

Why, then, was I not happy where I was? I could not tell. I only knew that I was restless, impatient, fidgety. I had a great curiosity about other things and other places. I did not know what I was looking for, but I had to find out. Something drove me, something

so strong that it drove me out of the jungle.

Time slipped by. It was a long wandering—a journey with many stops—in and out of a strange wilderness, across miles and miles of burning sand. Sometimes there were paths that wound into nothingness; sometimes there were paths that straightened themselves into roads. Finally there was a road that led into a little street. The street widened—and I entered a village.

I had never seen houses before, yet I could guess what they were for. Although I did not know why, they seemed inviting. The people who went in and out of them did not frighten me. Somehow, I knew that they would be part of my life and I would be part of theirs. What confused me was the smells. Some made me lick my lips with pleasure; some made me wrinkle my nose with disgust. I sniffed my way along the street and into the entrance of one of the houses. Suddenly I smelled something that made me tremble with excitement. I could not understand why I was quivering until what excited me took shape. It was small and brown; it had pointed ears and a long tail. I have no idea what made me do it, but I pounced on the thing, seized it by the neck, and shook it to death. The next thing I knew I was eating it.

People appeared all around me. I heard voices, and somehow I could understand what they were saying.

"Look!" cried one. "The wild thing has killed a mouse."

"Blessings on the creature, whatever it is," said another. "That mouse and a million like him have brought us nothing but trouble. Nothing—no food, no grain, no hidden thing—nothing is safe from them. They overrun the country, and they cannot be caught. They are too many and too quick for us."

"But not too quick for the wild thing," said the first voice. "Perhaps we could coax it to stay."

Before I had finished eating, they brought me a little bowl of milk. I had tasted milk before, but this was sweeter. I lapped it up eagerly. I purred my thanks.

"What a pretty sound," said a child. She came over and patted my head. I mewed softly.

"It answers!" cried the child. "It told me its name! It said 'Meoo.' I'm going to call it that. Here, Meoo! Come, Meoo!"

I rubbed against the child. She sat down and I settled myself in her lap.

"This is Meoo's home," she said. "Meoo's going to stay."

The child was right: I stayed. Her family became my family. Their friends became my friends; their enemies were my enemies. I did not wait for mice to appear; I went in search of them. I also learned how to hunt snakes and other slimy things that came out of the river. A bed of sweet-smelling straw was made for me, but I seldom used it. Whenever the child went to sleep I cuddled up beside her; she liked to feel me close to her body. Her bed was my bed.

One night while we were sleeping, something startled me awake. I did not know what it was, but I was aware that something peculiar was in the room, something evil. Then, in the dark, I could see it moving. It looked like a mouse, but much bigger; it smelled like a mouse, but much worse. It had red eyes and enormous teeth, and suddenly it jumped on the bed and sprang at the child. Before it could sink its teeth in the child's throat, I leaped on the creature. It did not collapse or try to run away like a mouse. It fought, and I fought with it; it was hideous and ferocious, and when it bit me, I used my claws. We struck and stabbed. We tore each other—the bed became a bloody mess—but I managed to throw its body to the ground and drag it to a corner; there I killed it.

The struggle must have been noisy, for as I gave a last triumphant

yowl, people came into the room. They did not look at me or the creature, but only at the bed and the child, who had been frightened awake and lay there moaning.

"The child!" screamed a woman. "She's covered with blood!"

Then she saw me. "And look!" she shrieked. "The child's pet did it—there's blood all over it! The thing is still wild! It must be destroyed!"

Someone ran from the room and came back with a knife. I was grabbed by the neck, and the knife was about to be thrust in my side when they saw the thing on the ground.

"A rat!" cried the woman. "A monstrous, blood-drinking rat! The cat killed it and got wounded. And we were ready to murder the creature who saved the child's life! Come, good Meoo. Let's see where you are hurt."

They picked me up tenderly. They washed me in warm water; they stopped the bleeding; they rubbed salve on my sores. They fed me fish and the most delicate pieces of meat; they crooned over me while I ate. They never stopped praising me. Never was a cat so coddled and cared for.

Did I say "cared for"? I was idolized. They put a fancy collar around my neck and couldn't stop talking about how beautiful and brave I was. Not only neighbors but people from far away came to stare and bring gifts. It was said that anyone who touched me would have good luck the rest of his life.

One day a visitor came who was unlike the others. He was tall and dark, and his face was stern. He wore a robe embroidered in gold, and on his head was a kind of crown in the shape of a falcon. He spoke to the head of the household.

"I am the High Priest of the temple in Nekheb," he said. "I have heard about your remarkable cat, and I have come for help. The people in my district are facing a famine. The crops are poor—they have been getting worse each year—and the supply of food is far too small for our needs. In the past we have always managed to keep stocks of corn and grain. Now there is nothing left. You can guess why."

"Mice," said the head of the household.

"Mice *and* rats," said the High Priest. "As our supply grew less, they increased in size and numbers. They breed by the time they are a few months old, and they have half a dozen litters a year. As I said, we need help badly. We need your cat."

That is how I became a temple cat. And that is how I founded a famous family. The High Priest had a cat of his own, but it was a feeble female. She too had come out of the jungle. But unlike me, she had not been happily domesticated. She would not rouse herself; she scarcely ate; she showed no interest in hunting. Mice ran under her nose and she never lifted a paw to stop them. The temple attendants had tried to cure her, but she refused to swallow the medicine they forced between her teeth. They had no idea what made her ill. I knew. She was sick with loneliness.

When the High Priest brought me into the temple, she arched her back. Then she spat. When I did not move, she growled and got to her feet as if she were going to stalk something suspicious. Coming closer, she stopped bristling; her ears, which had flattened against her head, stood up. Then, growing more curious, she sniffed my fur, sniffed again and again. Finally she rubbed a cheek against my side, and lay down beside me. I licked her chin.

Never had a cat found a lovelier mate, or a livelier one. She purred and pranced and ran with me everywhere I went. She hunted even more eagerly than I. In a week there was no sign of a mouse in the temple and no sign that she had ever been ill.

When the kittens came, she proved to be as wonderful a mother as she was a mate. She taught the little ones what was to be let alone and what was to be hunted, caught, and killed. They learned so quickly that the High Priest lent them to other temples. Their hunting grounds grew wider. They scoured the riverbank. They saved neighborhood after neighborhood. They cleansed every temple.

The High Priest summoned other priests from every corner of the country. Standing at the stone altar, he addressed them.

"We have every reason to be grateful to the cat who came out of the jungle. He and his offspring have rid our homes as well as our holy places of the pests that threatened our lives. He too is holy. When he or any of his kind happen to die, the people must shave their eyebrows as a sign of grief, embalm the body of the cat, wrap it in fine linen, and place it in a painted coffin. It must then be buried in the tomb belonging to its people."

He paused and lifted his right hand. "Hearken," he said. "The cat is to be reverenced, and anyone who kills it, even by accident, will be put to death. And this cat, father of our saviors, shall be seated among the gods and shall be worshiped as one of the greatest."

That was how it happened. They made many sacred images of me. Some were small and made of wood like toys, and children would murmur little prayers as they fondled their miniature gods. Some were larger than life-size; they were carved in ivory and stone and were placed in front of temples or at the gates of a city.

The favorite—the one that looked most like me—was the most beautiful. It was a seated figure made in bronze and it was called the Great God Bast. It had a collar of precious emeralds and turquoises, and a gold ring hung from the right ear. It was surrounded by smaller cats made of green bronze. And on certain feast days (it was said) you could hear all of them purr.

THE SECOND LIFE
HOW I SAVED MY COUNTRY

My second life took place in Persia, in a king's palace. It was a magnificent building, one of the wonders of the world. Actually, it was several buildings connected by glittering arcades and topped with domes of gold. There were five hundred rooms with arched doorways, and each room was furnished in different-colored silks. The walls were studded with jewels made into pictures of birds and animals. Glazed tiles of blue and yellow brought the sky indoors and carried the sun into every corner. My room was the king's room. When he sat on the throne I sat at his right side.

Perhaps I should tell you what I looked like. I was an entirely different kind of cat from the wild thing that came to be worshiped in Egypt. My body was covered with long hair of the purest white, and my tail was a silver plume. My head was round, my ears were small, and there was a ruff around my neck. My eyes were sapphire blue. The only other spot of color was my nose, which was as pink as the rosebuds in the royal gardens. I was, in every sense, a pure Persian, a true aristocrat.

I remember the day when I sat on my embroidered cushion next to the throne while cats of every kind and color were paraded before me. The king had decided that I should have a mate, and courtiers vied with merchants to present the finest breeds of all catdom.

The first that they brought in was a red tabby. Her coat, which was as long as mine, glistened. Her face was like the moon when, like a red ball, it rises over the eastern hills. Her eyes were deep copper.

"A beauty!" exclaimed the governor who had brought her. "Truly she is worthy to be matched with the favorite of the king of kings."

"She is red," replied the king. "Red is the color of anger, of blood and fire. It would not do to mix the red of violence with the white of innocence. Take her away."

The ambassador from Abyssinia opened a basket, and out jumped a long, sleek, amber-colored creature.

"This," said the ambassador proudly, "is our glory, the Abyssinian *Felis catus*. Her ancestors came from Africa and were noble. Notice that there is not a stripe or a spot on her velvet body; but the head has royal markings, and her tail is tipped with ebony. There is still some wildness in her blood, which makes her a queen among hunters."

"Pretty she is," said the king. "But there is a look in her eyes I distrust. We do not need hunters, and a wild thing is the last thing we want."

A merchant from Malaya came forth. "O king of kings," he said, "let me show you a cat that is both a criterion of courage and a curiosity. Observe," he continued, displaying a jet-black cat. "She is built differently from all other cats. It is said that she is part rabbit. Her fur is thicker than that of any other kind of cat, her leaps are quicker, and her tail can never be caught in a trap or disfigured in a fight because"—he smiled—"she has no tail."

The king returned the smile. "Unusual she is, and the rabbitlike stump is interesting. But we do not want our Persian to rear oddities. His match must be as perfect as he is."

"Behold," a voice said softly. "I have what your majesty has been seeking. I come from Siam, and no country has bred anything as lovely and love-worthy as the Siamese cat. No feline has equaled the sleekness of her fawn-colored body, graceful as any fawn in the forest. Her feet, ear-tips, and tail are pointed with blue. Her eyes too are bright with blue. Her voice is like no other's—deep, vibrant, alternately high and husky. Best of all, she is the most faithful of companions."

"You have spoken well," said the king. "The cat answers all my demands. The alliance between Persia and Siam will be strengthened by a union of these two courtly creatures. Moreover, a mating should bring out the noblest qualities of each. I look forward to the result with eagerness."

The king was not disappointed. My name was Pasha, so she was called Masha, and she bore the most beautiful as well as the most surprising of litters. All the kittens had the fawn-colored body, the gray-blue points, and the brilliant blue eyes of the Siamese, but they had—for the first time in the world—the long hair of the Persian.

The magicians were summoned, and their report justified the king's hopes.

"The omens could not be better," they said. "All the signs indicate that this new breed will yield secrets—secrets that can be revealed by those who can interpret them."

"Such as magicians, I suppose," said the king dryly.

"Your majesty is always right," said the chief magician, bowing his head. "It is we who will translate the secrets, but it is the cats who will show us what they know. It is through them that we will have the power to predict."

Day after day the magicians watched the kittens and reported what their behavior meant. When the kittens purred softly the magicians told the king that there would be a plentiful harvest and a long period of peace. When they stretched themselves they predicted that the workers would tend to be lazy and should be made to work faster on the new roads. When the kittens washed behind their right ear, the magicians foretold mild weather from the south. When the little ones scratched their left ear, the magicians warned about storms from the north.

One day the magicians presented themselves before the ruler in a state of great agitation.

"O king of kings," they said, "we are troubled. The kittens are meowing!"

"Is there anything strange about that?" inquired the king. "Isn't it natural for a kitten to mew?"

"To mew, yes," replied the chief magician. "But this is a loud cry, and a continual one. If only one kitten were complaining, we would make nothing of it. But all of them are raising their voices at once. And they will not stop. They will not eat. They will not be comforted. They are telling us what we must tell you."

"And what are they telling?"

"That your enemies are planning to overthrow your kingdom. That, even now, an Egyptian army is on the way. Having evaded the sentries, the vanguard has already crossed the frontier."

The generals were immediately summoned. They could not con-

ceal their alarm.

"O king of kings," said their commander, "these are terrible tidings. The Egyptians had sworn to be loyal; we have always treated them as allies, and we did little to protect the frontier. Before we decide what is to be done, we must learn the size of the invading army, its equipment, and its power."

Spies were sent out at once. Only a few returned. Their report was ominous. The Egyptian army was five times as large as the Persian. It was equipped with chariots, cavalry, and the fiercest archers. The food supply of a border city had been seized and its councilors taken prisoner.

"It is evident that they are prepared for a sudden attack and what they hope will be a short war," said the commander. "We must face the possibility of defeat unless we can come to terms with them."

"There can be no such 'unless,'" said the king. "The pride of the Persians will not permit giving in to traitors."

"If we cannot outfight them," said one of the captains, "we can outwit them. It is well known that cats are considered sacred by the Egyptians. If we were to face them with kittens in our arms they would not loose a single arrow against us. They would not risk injuring a single one of their cat-gods. It would be a sacrilege."

"No," said the king. "For one thing, using a kitten as a shield would be cowardly. For another thing, it would be only a defensive measure. We must punish the invaders, repel them, and drive them out of the country once and for all. If we are to use the cats, we will use them as we have previously done—as oracles. Go back to Pasha and his young ones," he said to the chief magician. "Study them again closely, but quickly. Report to me within the hour."

I had heard everything that had been said. I knew something had to be done, and I knew what to do. Before the magicians came, I ran to the kittens, who were huddled around Masha. I spoke to them.

"We cats have a sense of things to come. Dark clouds are over our country now; darker ones will follow. But there is a much greater darkness on the way—a darkness that will both help and hinder. Somehow we must make it known."

They understood. They lifted their voices, raised them higher than ever. When the magicians came they screamed and screeched, they cried and shrieked, they howled and yowled, they wailed and caterwauled. I joined them. So did Masha. Never was there such a noise. Then, at a sign from me, they stopped. All of them. All at once. They did not even breathe. Never was there such a silence.

The magicians were awed. They hurried back to the king.

"O king of all lands," they said, "we have listened to the Inspired Ones and they have told us what to expect. They let us know that there will come a darkness such as we have never known—a darkness like death. And it will happen when the sky is at its brightest. One moment the earth will be radiant with sunlight; then gradually the light will be withdrawn. The sun will disappear and the earth will be hushed. And this, they foretell, will happen Sunday, the day of the sun."

"That will be the time for us to attack," said the king. "The Egyptians have not been forewarned. They will be frightened by the growing blackness, and we will strike in the dark."

That is the way it happened. On Sunday morning everyone prayed to Mazda, the god who was called the Heavenly Glory. They prayed that the sun would turn his face away from the enemy but continue to shine on the worshipers of the life-giving Mazda. Then the king put himself at the head of his army, and with banners blowing and trumpets blazing, went to meet the Egyptians.

It was noon when the outposts sighted the enemy. The sky was

still bright, but something was happening to the sun. It was as if some unseen monster had taken a bite out of the celestial body. The bite grew in size; soon half of the sun was eaten up. Then the rest of the sun was blotted out and lost. Where the sun had been, weird streamers of flame shot across the sky. When they died down, stars appeared in all parts of the heavens. As the blackness increased, a chill fell over the earth.

The Egyptians were terrified. The soldiers were panic-stricken. Many ran aimlessly about; many were too paralyzed to move. The animals made the situation more frightful; they screamed, broke loose, and ran kicking among the troops. The havoc was indescribable.

Our men had been prepared for this. They flew to the attack. The darkness protected them as with their heads masked by heavy shields, they plowed into the Egyptian hordes. The enemy was overwhelmed; they broke for what little shelter they could find. The slaughter would have been horrible but for a miracle. Just as we were about to hack the enemy to pieces, a rim of light appeared, and the sun began to regain its place in the heavens. Even before the last of the darkness vanished, the enemy surrendered.

Attended by his chief generals, the Egyptian commander made his way to the king, who stood on a little hill beyond the battlefield. "We are your servants," he said. "No one can stand against a monarch who controls the sun. Let us depart to our homes, and let there be peace between our countries until the end of time."

Instead of humiliating his foe, the king forgave the enemy and sent the Egyptians back across the border with blessings. Never again was his power challenged or his rule troubled.

Back at the palace, he assembled his court. Ascending the throne and placing me beside him, he spoke. "We are to be congratulated," he began. "It was a great victory, all the greater because it was bloodless. We owe our triumph to Mazda, lord of light and life. We also owe not only our victory but our very lives to the one who conveyed Mazda's message, the precious being who sits at our right side."

He paused and patted me affectionately. Then he motioned to his councilors.

"This is our command," he said. "We decree that when this cat dies—and may that not happen for many, many years—a marble monument be erected in his honor. It shall show his image with a full sun carved behind him. And at the base these words shall be engraved: 'Sacred to Mazda and the memory of Peerless Pasha, the Cat Who Saved His Country.'"

THE THIRD LIFE
HOW I
LED AN ARMY

nlike my lives in Egypt and Persia, my life in Rome was a long and fierce struggle. Most Romans hated cats, and my master always had to defend himself because he not only kept me but cared for me. He was a butcher, and we lived in his shop, which was near the marketplace in the Campus Martius, not far from the Roman Forum. His friends never stopped annoying him about me. One evening they were particularly bitter.

"You should be ashamed of yourself," said Gaius the cobbler. "Everyone knows that cats are cowardly creatures. They are not companionable and faithful like dogs, but troublesome and treacherous."

"They are not to be trusted," chimed in Lepidus the porter. "Cats are foreigners—they came from Egypt, where the stupid people treated them like gods. They give themselves airs and act as if they expect to be worshiped here too."

"They don't belong here, that's sure," added Appius the plow-man. "We should get rid of them. All of them."

My master did not argue. All he said was, "He is my cat. He needs me. And I need him."

That was not the end, however. My master's neighbors stopped talking, but they did not stop planning. They set their dogs on me, but I was too quick for them; the curs chased me down the streets and through the alleys, but I sprang on walls and curled up on roofs, where they could not reach me. Poison was put in my food, but I could smell the venom before I tasted the stuff that would have killed me. They threw things at me—stones, broken bottles, and all kinds of filth—but although I was hit and sometimes hurt, I licked the cuts and healed the wounds; I even grew proud of my scars. But I was hounded by day and harried by night.

The worst was to come. They quit plaguing me and started to harm my master. Not only did they stop buying his meat, but they saw to it that nobody traded with him. They told anyone who came near the shop that what he said as well as what he sold turned people's stomachs. It did not take long to put my master out of business. He had to look for something to do, but rumors about his reputation had ruined him, and no one wanted to employ him. Unable to find work, he joined the army. I went with him.

For seven years we roamed all over Europe. The head of the army was a man named Julius Caesar. He did not act like a lord, superior to the men he led. On the contrary, he mingled with the soldiers as though he were one of them. He ate with them, joked with them, slept on the same kind of hard bed they did, and often marched along on foot with them. Unlike other generals, who gave orders but stayed safely behind the battle line, he was always at the front, leading his army into the thick of the fight. Everything he did was done like a companion, and his men adored him. They would have followed him to the end of the world and beyond, for he was not only a noble commander but also their comrade.

My master and I were with him when he raided Gaul and defeated a conspiracy of savage tribes. We went on to drive a German army across the Rhine. After sweeping through France, we invaded Britain and crossed the Thames; Caesar set up a Roman colony there. Everywhere we went I had new experiences. I lived with strange people and learned to eat strange foods. My nature changed. I had always been a timid cat—my early life in Rome had made me afraid of people and fearful of dogs. Now the rough life among soldiers toughened me; instead of being chased by dogs, I chased them. My master was proud of me, and I became the mascot of our company.

After seven years and countless victories it was time to return to Rome. Caesar's army, flushed with success, looked forward to a glorious homecoming. The men sang all the way to the border of Italy. There, on the north bank of a small stream, the Rubicon, Caesar stopped them. He addressed the troops.

"We are facing our homeland," he said. "We are also facing trouble. Word has come that jealous politicians and other powerful enemies have been plotting against me. They say that I must not enter Rome at the head of a victorious army, for if I do, the people may make me their emperor and take power away from my enemies. I will be permitted to enter Rome as a private citizen; but if I come with my troops, they will fight us. That means civil war, and as a son of Rome, that is the last thing I want. And yet——"

Caesar paused. The men looked at each other. Their leader had never hesitated before. They waited for his decision.

"There is our goal," he said. "Crossing the little bridge of that

small stream means our final triumph or our greatest failure. An army is drawn up on the south side. Shall we cross it?"

I did not see the army. But I saw a dog, a yellow dog, on the other side of the bridge. He was snarling, disputing the way, daring any living thing to approach.

I accepted the challenge. I leaped across the bridge and sprang at the mongrel's throat. He retreated so fast that he did not have time to howl.

"An omen!" cried Caesar. "A cat has decided for us. We cross the Rubicon!"

The troops swept over in irresistible waves. There was no way of stopping them. The enemy line broke, panicked, and disappeared. The road to Rome was open all the way.

Never had there been such a celebration. There were games and banquets, parades in the streets, contests in the Colosseum, and merrymaking everywhere. The festivities lasted for days.

At the height of the rejoicing, Caesar summoned my master.

"I appoint you head of my favorite legion," he said. "You have a strong face and strong arms. And you have something else that I envy, something I would like to possess."

"Whatever it is, O Caesar," said my master, "it is yours."

"No," said Caesar. "It is for you to keep, to look on with particular pride. After all"—and Caesar smiled—"it isn't every cat who can lead an army."

THE FOURTH LIFE
HOW I BECAME HUMAN

My fourth life was one of the strangest of all the nine lives. It was spent in Florence, the lovely Italian City of Flowers. My master, who had lost his parents in childhood, had been brought up by an aunt. She had left him a considerable fortune, a town house, and a favorite cat, who happened to be me. His mother had been a famous beauty, and his father a noted doctor who, it was said, had cured more patients with magic than with medicine. He had had an enormous library of mysterious books about spells, sorcery, witchcraft, and all sorts of wonder-working.

My master's name was Filippo, and he was the handsomest youth to be found on either side of the river Arno. Wherever he went he was the center of attention. Men envied his fine features and the way he carried himself, gracefully but manfully, proudly but not pompously. Girls blushed when he spoke to them and looked back at him over their shoulders when he passed by. But he cared little that he was esteemed by men and not at all that he was sought after by women. He liked living alone—alone and (although it may sound boastful) with me. He was happiest on winter evenings when we both sat in front of the glowing fireplace or I dozed on his lap.

He loved to talk to me, and although I could not converse with him in his own language, I replied in my own way. I purred when I agreed with him, meowed when I disagreed or asked a question, and rubbed against him whenever I wanted attention. It was a daily communication, but it did not satisfy my master.

"If we could only talk, *really* talk, to each other," he would sigh from time to time. "What a wonderful companion you would make. If only there were some way!"

Then one night he clapped his hand to his forehead and sprang out of his chair. "There *is* a way!" he cried. "I was not born to be the son of a magician for nothing!"

He dragged book after book down from his father's library, turned over the pages, and excitedly copied what he thought he needed. He brought herbs from the garden, salt and spices from the larder, and something that I couldn't see but I knew was alive. He poured wine and water into a glass retort, added a powder, and heated the vessel until it turned many colors. He made a heart-shaped thing out of wax and dropped it into the mixture. Then he sprinkled ashes on the ground, drew a circle around them, and put me in the center.

"Now you must do your part," he said. "You must drink the colored mixture. It will not hurt you. It will put you to sleep. While you sleep, I will recite spells, weave charms, and do certain things that have to be done. You will know nothing about what is taking place, but when you wake you will no longer be a cat. You will be a

human being—a boy, a young man my own age. And we will be comrades as long as we live."

I did as I was told. I drank the mixture—it tasted queer but not unpleasant—and I fell asleep. I had strange dreams, but they had no connection with anything at all. I remember only that I was wakened when I heard my master shout.

"It worked!" he cried. "It worked!"

A moment later his cry of joy became a cry of distress. "It worked, but not the way I planned it! I must have forgotten something, and it's too late to add or change anything. What have I done!"

What he had done was not what he intended. He had certainly performed magic, and he had definitely changed me. But instead of transforming me into a boy, he had turned me into a girl!

He was stunned. His face was white; his eyes went blank; he seemed to stop breathing. But he was not the sort that is depressed for long. He looked at me sadly and said, "I wish it had turned out differently. But complaining won't help. We must make the best of it. Yes?"

He waited for a reply. But although I tried, I could not utter a word.

"What's the matter?" he said anxiously. "Has anything else gone wrong? Could I have forgotten something again?"

He had, indeed, forgotten an important something. Besides the mistake of making me into a girl, he had forgotten the precious ingredient that was to give me the power to talk. I was speechless. I could not even mew.

"And we were going to have such good conversations together!" He groaned.

My eyes expressed what my tongue could not say. They showed how sorry I was.

"Will you ever forgive me?" he said. "I'll never forgive myself. Still, we must face the facts. What's done is done. As I said, we must make the best of the situation. At least we must try. Now that you are a woman, I will have to learn to live with you. And you will have to learn to live with me. But how? What can you do?"

I found out that I could do everything that any woman could do. I kept house for him. I cooked his meals, tidied up his room, put fresh linen on his bed, mended his socks, played cards with him, and listened while he read to me. I put flowers on the breakfast table. I did everything to make myself not only necessary but also more attractive to him. Sometimes I piled my hair high on top of my head like a crown; sometimes I arranged it in two long braids tied with bright ribbons; sometimes I let it fall in waves beneath my shoulders almost to my waist. I learned that his favorite colors were green and blue, so I wore nothing but green and blue dresses, or clothes that were a combination of the two. I made myself small shell earrings and a necklace of little bells, for he loved the sound of light music. I realized I was completely a woman when I felt he was falling in love with me.

"I would never have believed it," he said one evening as he put down his book. "It is a double miracle. I never cared for a woman — and now you are the only thing I care for. I never knew what people meant when they spoke of love." He stopped, then said, "Do you feel what I feel?"

He rose and held out his arms. I walked into them.

And so we were married.

I have been told that silent women make the best wives. It seemed to be true in my case, for although I never spoke a word, no man and wife could have been happier. We shared every moment, and every moment was golden. We were always together. We played together; we worked together, he at his chores and I at mine. We ate, walked, played, and slept together.

One night in spring when we were sleeping a strange thing happened. I woke suddenly, wide awake, with the feeling that an unseen something was in the room. My whole body trembled. But it was not fear that me quiver. I was startled to realize that I was trembling with anticipation, with something like joy. It was a sensation that I seemed to have experienced long before, a lifetime before. In a flash I knew what it was. I knew what made me sit up with such tense excitement. It was a mouse.

I did not scream as women are supposed to do. Instead I quietly left my bed, crept silently across the room, crouched, pounced, and seized the mouse in my teeth. I shook it until it was dead, and then I ate it to the last morsel. It was delicious.

Licking my fingers, I went calmly back to bed without disturbing my husband.

"And how did you sleep?" he asked me, as he always did in the morning.

I smiled as if to say, "Never better."

He patted my hand. "You smile as though you were remembering a pleasant dream. Was it so delightful?"

I licked my lips. Then I kissed his cheek.

After that, life went on as usual. But every once in a while I would be wakened by the sound of a rustling in the walls, or a light scampering in the attic, or a little something gnawing in the corner. Then I would sit up, my blood would race, and I would wait eagerly until some instinct told me it was time. I never planned the hunt—I never knew when it might happen—but I never missed.

My dear husband knew nothing of my irregular midnight meals. He never suspected that I relished an occasional change of diet. Over and over again he told me how happy I made him.

"I am the luckiest man in the world," he said. "And you are the loveliest of women."

I smiled and prevented myself from purring.

"Yes," he continued, "you are not only the quietest and dearest but also the most wonderful woman that ever lived. The magic was perfect. It is hard for me to believe—and I am sure you cannot possibly remember—that you ever were such a thing as a cat."

I smiled again. I was glad that I could not talk. Had I been able to talk, I would have had to tell the truth—I never could tell a lie— and the truth would have hurt him.

As a matter of fact, I hurt him without telling the truth. As time went on he began to notice things, things that puzzled him. One morning he pointed to something on the floor. It was a half-eaten mouse.

"I don't suppose you have any idea how it got there," he said. "Could a cat have come into our bedroom? And if so, how? The slightest noise would have wakened you, yet you slept soundly through the night."

I rubbed against him as a kind of reassurance. But I could see that he was troubled. Then one night I failed to catch a mouse and I had a bad time. I was restless. I dreamed that I was being attacked and had to defend myself. I woke when my husband jumped from the bed and cried out in pain. He was bleeding. There were scratches all over his body.

He looked at me queerly. For the first time, he sensed that something was wrong.

"There are things about you, my darling, that I don't understand," he said. "I'm beginning to suspect that there's been a change in your nature. Some mornings you are so hungry you can't wait until breakfast; other mornings you won't touch anything on the table. You drink

more and more milk and—if I may say so without offending you—you drink it, or lap it, rather noisily. I may be mistaken, but I could swear that I have heard you growl in your sleep."

What could I do? I put my arms around him and held him close. I wept. I could not stop the tears.

"Don't cry," he said. "It's my fault that you are unhappy. Perhaps I should change you back to what you used to be."

I shook my head and hugged him tighter.

"Never mind," he said. "I love you as you are. Besides," he added with a rueful smile, "I'm not sure I could do it. I don't want to make another mistake—especially since my first mistake brought me you. I've always heard that there's something of a woman in every cat and something of a cat in every woman. Who am I to change that? I wouldn't change it even if I could. What keeps us together is that we love one another. And no matter what, we always will."

His were the right words, right for both of us. He loved to talk and I loved to listen. We lived the rest of our lives that way, happily (as they say in the storybooks) ever after.

THE FIFTH LIFE
HOW I MADE FRIENDS WITH MICE

My fifth life was a wild one. It took place four hundred years ago, and it was spent on the wild west coast of Brittany. This was a weird part of France, a vast peninsula that jutted far out into the Atlantic. Everything about it was queer. There were long rows of huge upright stones that had been put up ages and ages before men built houses. These crudely chiseled boulders were given unusual names—"megalith" and "menhir" and "cromlech"—and they were part of some primitive ceremony that remained a mystery. There were older monuments too, thousands of ancient rock chambers roofed with flat rocks, and cavelike hollows, which served as burial places. The interiors were carved and painted in honor of the all-powerful goddess the Earth Mother. And as though nature intended to imitate the works of man, the sea had sculptured the rocks along the shore into unearthly shapes.

The people were as singular as their surroundings. They were a superstitious lot. They believed, as their forefathers had done, in spirits, mostly evil, that controlled the world; and their lives were almost as wild as the countryside. Their dress was contrary. They wore coarse capes and heavy, broad-brimmed hats in summer, and freakishly flimsy caps in winter. Most of them lived in rough stone houses with thatched roofs, and their sheep and cattle lived in the houses with them. Wiry and hard, they had mean minds and sullen natures that could turn ugly when opposed. They were particularly wary of my master, the old count who lived in what remained of a castle on the edge of the town.

Once, long ago, the castle had been a noble stronghold. But over the centuries, time and storms from the sea had reduced it to ruins. A tower had been left standing, but my master and I lived in a few rooms that were still held up by oak beams, and he had reinforced the rotted sills with strong timber. In his day my master had been a famous fighter, but he had lost two sons in battle and he had sworn never to fight again. He had burned his combat clothes and melted down his armor to make tools. He used his iron helmet as a kettle. The only reminder of his past was a sword so sharp that, people said, it could cut through steel and had a shine capable of blinding enemies. Now dulled and rusted, it stood in a corner of the hearth and was used only to poke up the smoldering fire.

The place was overrun with animals, chiefly mice and rats. But my master, who loved all living things, did not mind them. Neither did I. In my earlier lives mice had been my natural prey. Not only had I hated them, but I had hunted them, caught them, and eaten them without a thought. In this life, instead of despising or devouring them, I pitied them. I actually got to be fond of them. After all, it was not their fault that they were mice. What harm did they really do? Mice, it is said, are thieves. But what do they steal? A crumb or two, a left-over bit of bacon, a scrap of cheese that no one wanted to eat. As I say, I got to be friends with the mice that scurried around the rooms. I told them my troubles, and they told me theirs.

Troubles there were, and plenty of them. Things had been quiet for some time, but the townspeople were not a peaceful people. They quarreled with their neighbors and made enemies of friends. Naturally hostile, they were always looking for a pretext to start a fight. Rumors that men in a nearby village were conspiring gave them the excuse they needed. Whenever I went along the street I could hear them plotting. They talked of nothing else.

"We must prepare for action," said one. "We have been idle too long. We have grown soft."

"We must do more than prepare," said another. "We must attack. Offense is the best kind of defense."

"I agree," said a third. "The whole town agrees. We have everything we need for war except one thing. We need a leader."

This presented a problem for discussion. But there was no argument. Everyone concurred that there was only one man experienced enough to lead them, and that man was my master, the old count.

"But," said one of the townsmen, "he has retired from all activities and does not like to be disturbed."

"We will take him out of retirement," said another. "It will stir up his blood."

"But," said the first, "he has sworn never to fight again."

"It was a foolish oath," said the second.

"Yes," said a third. "We will persuade him that he was wrong. And," he added grimly, "there are ways to persuade him."

I hurried home, but I had not been there more than an hour before a crowd came to the castle. At the head of it was the man who had spoken last. He called himself a captain and acted as spokesman for the crowd. He knocked on the door. My master opened it. I was at his heels.

"What is it you want?" asked my master.

"We want you," was the answer. "We are in danger. We must strike first, and you must show us how to do it."

"Who has harmed you?" inquired my master.

"No one—yet. But there are people in the next town whom we distrust. We don't like the way they talk or the way they look. They do not think like us. We should teach them a lesson."

"You have come to the wrong man," said my master. "For one thing, I never would join a pack of bullies. For another, I gave up fighting years ago. War proves nothing except that people get killed. And none of the talk about glory and honor is ever a comfort to the dead, or to those who mourn them."

"You talk like a coward," said the captain. "Shouldn't we take risks to get what we need, what we want?"

"There is plenty here for everyone. The teeming earth, the fertile fields, the rich harvests—all are generous, all are good. But peace, peace among men, is best of all."

"Enough of preaching. Will you join and lead us?" The captain's voice was hard. "Yes or no?"

"No," said my master. "That is the end of it."

"You are mistaken," said the captain. "It is not the end. If you are not with us you are against us. And anyone who opposes us is our enemy. You will see."

My master did not bother to reply to the threat. He entered the castle calmly and I hurried after him. After he had settled down with one of his large books, I summoned my friends the mice. I told them to call their cousins, the rats. When they were all assembled, I spoke.

"Something is going to happen, something that may affect all our lives. Can I depend on you?"

They all nodded their heads, and I went on.

"An evil lot of men want to drag my master off to war. He has refused, and they are going to make war on him. We who live here must help him. Those men will come armed. But we are not defenseless. We too have weapons. We have teeth and claws. Sharpen them. You know how to use them when the time comes."

The time came sooner than I expected. The day had been dismal, but the night was drearier. The skies were clouded and bleak; there was storm in the air. Gloomy-looking men began to gather in front of the castle; by eleven o'clock there was a mob. It was hard to tell what they were doing; but a few of them had lanterns, and I could see that others were carrying branches and bundles of what looked like straw. There must have been fifty or more in the crowd when their spokesman raised his voice.

"Count, you have shut your mind against us. Now you have shut your door. Well, we will smoke you out."

There was a growl of thunder, and the man spoke louder.

"We have seen to it that the door is shut for good—our good. We have barred it with chains, and we have piled wood against the walls. We will give you one more chance to join us. If you still refuse, straw will be lighted, and the wood will begin to smoke. I need not tell you that where there is smoke there is fire. What is your decision?"

There was no reply. We knew what they intended to do. They were going to make a bonfire of the castle and burn up all that happened to be inside it. There was a moment's pause. The straw was lighted and a branch crackled. Then, as crashing thunder shook the earth, the whole sky lighted up and revealed my master at the door. In his hand was the old sword, but it was no longer rusted. He raised it

above his head and drove it through the door and through the chains that held the door. He flung the door open, and an army of mice and rats, with me at their head, poured through. We dashed into the straw, scattering the flames. A wind blew the sparks toward the mob, and we rushed along as though we had been raised on fire. Then we used our weapons.

There was shouting and screaming. "Look out for those blazing red eyes!" "They are fiends!" "They have teeth like knives!" "They are the evil ones, spirits out of hell!"

The panic grew greater as a flash of lightning showed my master still holding the sword, which shone so blindingly that no one could look at it.

"You wanted to unleash the dogs of war," he said scornfully. "But you are the dogs. Back to your kennels!"

The mob broke up. The men slithered away. There was no fight left in any of them, no more talk of war. A huge downpour of rain dampened the last thought of violence.

We could not call it peace, but we had brought about a truce that lasted. We were never troubled again.

THE SIXTH LIFE
HOW I
CREATED
A KING

You may not believe what I am going to tell you about my sixth life. Sometimes I do not believe it myself. It all seems so fantastic, so unreal. I was a cat and yet I was not a cat. For one thing I was incredibly large. When I stood up on my hind legs—and standing up was my favorite position—I was as tall as a man—well, as big as a growing boy. For another thing, I could talk. In fact I could talk as well as any of the lords and ladies, and (if I may say so) I could not only outtalk but also outthink any of them. They all admitted that I was a remarkably clever cat.

But though I became the darling of the court, I did not begin as a pampered pet in a lordly mansion. On the contrary. I was brought up—or rather, I brought myself up—in a broken-down mill. There were four people living in the mill, an old miller and his three sons. They lived poorly. The miller was old and feeble; the two older sons, who were lazy and shiftless, treated their young brother shamelessly. They let me stay in the mill because I kept the mice out of the flour bin, but they took pleasure in kicking me whenever I was within reach of their feet. Only the youngest son took pity on me. He fed me scraps from the little food they gave him, and at night we kept each other warm in bed.

One day the old miller called the three sons to his side.

"I have not long to live," he said, "and I have little to leave. I need no lawyer to make out a will. To you, my oldest son, I leave the mill—and may you do better with it than I did. The donkey that carries the ground corn to the market—when there is any to sell— belongs to you, my second son. As for my youngest, poor boy, there is really nothing for you."

The boy tried to comfort the old man. "Don't fret, Father," he said. "There is the cat. And if I take good care of the cat, someday," he added with a sad little laugh, "perhaps the cat will take care of me."

Little did he know that he spoke the truth. And little did I know how true it was to be.

A few weeks later the miller died. The oldest son took over the mill, the second gave the donkey some oats, and the youngest looked sorrowfully at me.

"What am I going to do with you?" he said. "I love you too much to sell you to someone who might buy you for the sake of your skin. Besides, I doubt if there's any demand for cat's fur these days. What will I do?"

He was a sweet boy but not very bright. I had to cheer him up.

"Don't worry," I said. "We'll get along somehow. In fact I have a plan, and I need only two things."

"You are a smart cat," he said. "I've watched how you caught mice by pretending you were dead or asleep, and how you managed to hide yourself in the flour bin. But what two things will help us?"

"A bag," I said, "and a pair of boots."

"I can see the reason for a bag, if we find anything," he said. "But boots?"

"Boots," I replied. "Boots are part of the plan. I expect to do a lot of walking, and the pads of my feet are very tender."

Three days later my young master brought me the things I had asked for. I don't know how he was able to get them, but get them he did. The boots fitted perfectly—I strutted around in them with great pleasure—and I hung the bag around my neck. "I may be gone for a while," I said. "But don't worry about me. I'll have something good to report when I return."

Then I went out into the fields where wild lettuce and sweet fennel grew. I tore some up with my teeth and stuffed it into the bag. Then, leaving the bag open, I lay down on the ground and pretended to go to sleep. Soon a rabbit poked his nose in the bag, liked what he smelled, wriggled in, and began to nibble. Before he knew what was happening, I pulled the string tight. Then I hung the bag around my neck again and trotted off. After a while I came to the border of the neighboring country and to the king's palace.

"I have a gift for his majesty," I said to the armed men at the gate.

"Of all things!" cried one of the guards. "A cat that speaks!"

"What's so wonderful about that?" said another. "Parrots can talk. Why not cats?"

The first guard shook his head, grumbled a bit, and led me into the palace. The attendants were astonished, but no one stopped me on my way to the royal apartment. The king stared when I stood before him, but he was too aristocratic to show surprise.

"Your majesty," I said, bowing, "I bring you a gift from my country. It is a rare kind of rabbit from the fields of my master,"—I suddenly thought of a fine-sounding title—"the marquis of Carabas."

The king was puzzled. He had never heard of any place called Carabas. But he was a shrewd monarch, and he thought that there might come a time when he would need the help of a marquis. He smiled graciously.

"Thank your master, the marquis," he said. "Tell him I am pleased with his thoughtfulness as well as his gift."

I bowed and left the royal presence. When I returned home, my master was curious and a little anxious.

"Where have you been?" he asked. "And what have you been doing?"

"Nowhere and nothing in particular," I said airily. "Something has been started, but it's too early to talk about it. When the time comes you will know all about it."

He sulked a little—I told you he was not too bright—but there was nothing more to say.

A few days passed, and once again I went into the fields. This time the bag was half filled with kernels of corn I had found in the mill. I hid among the tall grass, which was often visited by partridges. Soon a couple of the birds flew into the open bag. I tightened the string, and once again I carried my catch to the palace.

"Good morning," I said to the guards. Not only did they say, "Good morning to you," but they saluted me. The attendants were too polite to question me further. I was accepted by all, including the king.

"What is it this time?" he asked as I placed my offering before him.

"I bring you high-bred partridges from my master's game pre-

serves," I said. "Carabas is famous for its specially fed wild fowl."

"Thank your master again," said the king. "He must be a man of excellent taste."

Things went on like this for two months. Once a week, and sometimes more often, I would present the king with quail, ruffed grouse, ptarmigan, a pheasant, or some other game. The king continued to accept the gifts with his usual grace. But though he was too courteous to inquire, I could see that he was wondering.

"Your master must be an interesting man," he said. "I would like to meet him. I assume he is young. If he is, I would also like him to meet my daughter, who, I am told, is the most beautiful princess in the world. As a matter of fact, she and I and a few courtiers are going on a little outing this afternoon. We will be riding along the river that divides our two countries. Perhaps the marquis might be doing something of the sort. It promises to be a lovely day."

I hurried home. "The time has come," I told my master. "You must go at once to a place along the riverside."

"Why?" he asked.

"Don't ask questions," I said. "Just follow me and I will tell you what to do."

When we came to a certain spot, we stopped.

"Now what?" he said.

"Now," I said, "take off your clothes and jump in the river, swim around a little, and when I give the signal, cry out."

He had not been in the water more than a few minutes when the king and his daughter came along. I gave the signal, my master cried out, and I shouted, "Help! Help! My master, the marquis of Carabas, is drowning!"

The king's company came to a halt. The monarch immediately recognized me and ordered the courtiers to the riverbank.

They had no trouble pulling the marquis from the water.

"How fortunate that you happened to be passing," I told the king. "My master came here to refresh himself after a hot ride. While he was swimming he became so excited that he started to drown. Some thieves had stolen his horse and all his clothes. He saw them and shouted. I tried to stop them, but the robbers were too quick for me."

Of course there was no horse, and I had hidden my master's shabby clothing beneath a rock. The king sent his courtiers back to the palace.

"Bring a suit of the very finest, something fit for a marquis," he said. "With plenty of gold braid."

During this episode the princess had discreetly looked the other way. But when my master had been dressed in the rich raiment, she gave him a glance. It turned out to be much more than a glance. Her eyes opened wide; then her eyelids drooped; then they opened into a look of frank admiration. He returned her gaze, shyly but warmly. His usually pale cheeks grew red. She too blushed.

The king could not help but notice this. "Perhaps," he said, smiling, "the marquis would not object to coming back with us. It is only a short ride from your part of the country to the palace."

The royal carriage was brought up. The princess made a place for my master next to her, and he beckoned to me to come with them.

"Later," I told him. "There is something I must do first."

Putting my boots to work, I ran ahead of them and came to a rich meadow where men were mowing. Knowing that the king's company must pass it on the way back to the palace, I called out to them.

"My good fellows, do me a favor, and I'll do one for you. The royal carriage will soon pass here. If the king should ask who owns this land, tell him it belongs to the marquis of Carabas. Do that, and you will be rewarded."

They agreed, and when the royal carriage came along and the king inquired, the mowers said, "The meadow and everything on this side of the river belongs to our lord, the marquis of Carabas."

Farther on, there was a wide field that was being reaped. I said the same thing to the reapers, and they made the same reply when the king inquired.

"I must compliment you on your estate," the king said to my master. "Your lands must yield a rich harvest, and I am amazed that one so young has such fields, such meadows, and such a famous game preserve."

I overheard, but I hurried on. There was something still for me to do, and I knew where it had to be done. I was bound for a formidable castle owned by a huge ogre, the richest ogre that ever was, for all the lands that the royal carriage had passed through belonged to him. It was a splendid building with a wide moat, an iron drawbridge, and five magnificent towers. I had no trouble entering, for the ogre was so fearful in appearance and his power was so great that he needed no guards to protect him. He received me with a courtesy that did not conceal his curiosity.

"I have come to pay tribute to a mastermind," I said. "You are famous not only for your wealth but for your unsurpassed command of magic. I myself have done some conjuring, but on a very small scale. If I hear correctly, you can transform yourself into any shape, no matter how large. Is that true?"

"Of course it is true," he said sharply. "Would you like me to prove it? You would? Well, what would you like me to turn myself into?"

"What about a lion?" I said.

A moment later a lion with a bristling mane ran roaring about the room.

"Wonderful!" I exclaimed as the ogre resumed his true form. "Now can you make yourself into an even bigger animal—say an elephant?"

The ogre did not bother to reply. Before my eyes he became enormous, sprouted a mammoth trunk with two immense tusks, and filled the air with fierce trumpeting.

"Marvelous!" I cried. "Marvelous! I never would have believed it could be done. But can you do something even harder? You are so large, so heavyset a wizard, I wonder if you could possibly change yourself into something little, something very small."

"How small?" he said. "Like what?"

"Like—well, like a mouse," I said.

The ogre was just as stupid as I had expected. He began to shrink . . . and shrink . . . and shrink. As soon as he had changed himself into a mouse, I pounced on him. He made a very light meal. I did not like the taste.

I waited. Before the king and his company could return to his kingdom, they had to travel on our side of the river. When the royal carriage appeared on its roundabout way, I was standing on the drawbridge.

"We have been expecting you," I said. "Welcome, your majesty, to the ancient home of my master, the marquis of Carabas."

The king, with my master and the princess hand in hand, entered. Fortunately everything was ready for them. The ogre had arranged a banquet for certain of his fellow monsters whom he intended to invite, so we all sat down to a lavish feast. The king kept calling attention to the food, the furnishings, and the noble size of the castle, while the princess could not take her eyes off my master. Finally, after toasting my master several times, the king cleared his throat and made a short speech.

"It is not often that a monarch is entertained by so charming a subject," he said. "And, I may add, by such a modest one. If you have a request to make of me, speak up. Do not be afraid. Any request will be granted, including," he ended with a broad smile, "the hand of my daughter, who has not uttered a word, but"—he hiccupped—"her looks speak for her."

There was nothing more to say except what the lovers said to each other. They said it over and over again.

The next day was declared a national holiday. There were parades, games, and all sorts of entertainment. The festival lasted for a week, at the end of which my master and the princess were united in the most glorious marriage ceremony the country had ever seen.

Three years later the king died, and his son-in-law, the marquis, became potentate. His rule was benevolent; he rewarded everyone. Never had a monarch been so beloved, and never had a cat been so proud. There was good reason for my pride. I was the first cat in history to create a king.

There was only one thing that made me rather sad. I lost my appetite for mice. The taste of that ogre had turned my stomach.

THE SEVENTH LIFE
HOW I RODE ON A BROOMSTICK

My seventh life was really two lives, and both of them were spent in Weggis, a little town in Switzerland. I was not a beautiful nor even an unusual-looking cat. My color was plain gray, and my eyes were commonplace green. But my coat was so sleek and my fur so shiny that my mistress, an old, old lady, called me Silky. She gave me her love and everything that a cat could desire.

During the day, I would go walking with her along a stream that flowed into Lake Lucerne or sit silently by her side while she did the household chores. At night, however, I was not so quiet. In the dark, roaming along the rooftops, I became a strolling poet. I would sing the wildest love songs at the top of my voice, and many were the lady cats who listened and sighed, and many were the tomcats who envied me.

One day my pleasant life came to a sudden end. My mistress

died and I was left an orphan, an orphan who was unwanted. The old lady's heirs, two rough nephews, turned the place upside-down and ruined it. They never bothered to feed me, much less pet me. On the contrary, they called me ugly names and flung all sorts of things at me. They took what they wanted, boarded up the house, and threw me out into the street.

Then began my other life. I had to beg for food, hunt small, unsavory mice, and dig hungrily for greasy scraps that in my mistress' day would have disgusted me. I had no pride. When instead of giving me something to eat some mean man would yank my tail, I would not spit or scratch. Instead I would look longingly at the hand that hurt me but had such a good smell of sausage or herring. I, who had been plump, grew thin and scraggly. My shining fur became dull, matted, and dirty.

I was starving when a strange and somewhat sinister-looking man dropped a juicy morsel at my feet. I knew who he was. He was Mirvin, the town magician. My mistress had often spoken scornfully of him. He was a miser, a schemer, a smooth hypocrite. He called himself a learned wizard and claimed he could cure people of all their ills, especially of ills they had never had. He sold bottles of a curiously colored, queer-tasting drink that he guaranteed would stop coughs, remove warts, kill cockroaches, beautify the skin, restore strength to the weak, and make anyone fall in love with the buyer. The front of his house was like an ordinary druggist's, but it was in the back room that he made his peculiar kind of magic.

As soon as I devoured what he had dropped, he spoke to me.

"They used to call you Silky, didn't they?" he said. "No one would think of calling you that today. I will give you a new name, a name that fits you the way you are now. I will call you Slinky, the cat that has to slink and sneak and skulk in order to live. Yet, shabby and

poor though you are, you have something I would like, something I need. I would like to buy your fat."

I was not sure I understood what he had said. I sat and stared.

"Can't you hear me?" he said. "I want an answer. And"—he clapped his hands three times and made a kind of sign—"I hereby give you the power of speech. Speak up, now. What do you say?"

Astonished to find words coming out of my mouth, I answered, "Mirvin, the town magician, is making fun of me. It is cruel fun, because he knows there isn't an ounce of fat on my whole body."

"I can remedy that," said Mirvin. "I need cat's fat in my business. It's as important to a wizard as the eye of a newt, the leg of a lizard, the tongue of a snake, or the toe of a toad. I'll make you a good offer for your fat. I must have your consent and I'll make it worthwhile. If ever a cat was in a position to make a bargain, you are that cat."

"What," I said weakly, "can you do for your part of the bargain?"

"Never mind what I *can* do," said Mirvin. "I'll tell what I *will* do. I will make you finer and fatter than you have ever been. You will drink the richest milk, munch on the tenderest meat, crunch the crunchiest little bones, and lick the most delectable platters. You will feast and flourish on liver dumplings, kidneys in cream, stuffed quail, and potted pigeons."

"But," I said, "on such a diet I would die of indigestion."

"I will take care of that," said Mirvin. "I will see that you get plenty of exercise to keep you healthy and stimulate your appetite. Grass grows on my roof, long, lush, green grass. You will romp in it and imagine yourself a tiger in the jungle. Around the house there are all sorts of holes and crannies to explore, nooks in which you will find new and wonderful things to chivvy and chase. There will be plenty of hunting, but you won't have to hunt too hard. My mice are not only the juiciest but also the slowest mice in the world. And, oh, yes, in the back of my garden there is a thick growth of pure catnip. Again I ask, what do you say?"

"Well," I replied, my mouth watering, "it sounds very interesting. But there's one thing I don't understand. If I have to give you my fat, I will lose my life. And if I lose my life, how can I enjoy all those things when I am dead?"

"Don't be stupid," said Mirvin. "A bargain is a bargain. As long as you live—and you *may* live a long time—your life will be an endless feast. More you can't ask. Still"—he shrugged his shoulders and started to walk away—"I don't want to force you. Forget what I've said. Stay the way you are."

"Wait a minute," I said anxiously. "Give me a moment to think."

"Take your time," said Mirvin. "But be quick about it."

I thought fast. "All right," I said. "You can have my fat *and* my life on one condition. You are not to do anything to me until I am myself again, the fattest and silkiest self. Then you must give me three days more, three days of grace. I don't want to be torn away from all pleasure at the height of my enjoyment. I must have those extra three days."

"Very well," said Mirvin. "I accept the condition. I will give you a whole month and three days more. That will take us to the next full moon. After that——"

"I know," I said. "After that, my fat is yours."

With that understanding I moved into the house of Mirvin the magician. There were countless things to see, to smell, to taste, and to eat. I sampled everything. For a while I did nothing but gorge. I could not wait to stuff myself from one meal to the next, and between meals I nibbled. Mirvin had prepared delicacies I had never dreamed of—sardines fried in butter, sparrows stewed in oil, mice broiled in bacon.

I ate and ate and ate. And when I stopped eating I slept. Never had a cat slept so soundly, so contentedly, so blissfully. In a couple of weeks I was sleek and round and ever so lazy. The mice made fun of me. They ran around my pillow, and some of them came so close that their tails brushed my whiskers. But I paid no attention. I did not even lift a paw in protest.

Then one day as I was devouring a partridge that Mirvin had fattened, a thought struck me. I was destroying a bird that must have relished his rare tidbits and rich morsels—for what? He had stuffed himself, happily, heedlessly, as I was doing, for a miserable end. Suddenly I realized what a fool I'd been. What greedy, thoughtless, senseless fool! I knew something had to be done before it was too late. The answer was simple. I had to stop eating.

It was not easy, but stop I did. At least I stopped eating Mirvin's fancy foods. I determined to get rid of my fat before Mirvin got it. I refused to indulge myself, to cram delicious dainties and lie around on soft pillows. I raced through the streets, and when I was worn out I would lie on some hard stone. Instead of sitting down to a crisply browned bird, I hunted tirelessly, and the taste of a thin wild mouse was better than all the appetizers that came from Mirvin's kitchen. I sprang from roof to roof. A snow-white puss was washing herself on one of the gutters. She met my glance with a modest but encouraging meow. Before I reached her side, three other cats descended on me. There was a terrific battle. I lost part of an ear; there was blood all over my paws; my fur was torn and dirtied. But I had won my lady, and though every night there were savage fights with my rivals, I stayed with her for a week.

When I came home I looked tougher and thinner than ever. Mirvin was furious.

"You ragamuffin!" he screamed. "You bag of bones! You ugly,

ungrateful beast! So that is the way you try to cheat me! Well, we shall see what we shall see!"

I saw. A moment later it was plain what he meant to do. He went to the kitchen cupboard, pulled out a long knife, and began to sharpen it.

"Now, my fine fellow," he said, "we will wait no longer. The moon is full, and I shall take what little fat is left on you. It is much less than I had the right to expect, but there is a little. Besides, your skin will make a nice warm cap and maybe a pair of gloves. Now for your last words. Is there anything you'd like to say while you can still say it?"

"Yes," I said, "and I'm ashamed to say what it is. Because I didn't trust you I broke a promise."

"What are you talking about?" said Mirvin. "What kind of a promise?"

"Before my dear mistress died she hid a thousand gold pieces in a certain place. She made me promise to tell no one about it until I found the right man and the right girl. When that happened I was to give the treasure to the couple for a wedding present. Now it's too late."

"It's never too late to do the right thing," said Mirvin. "What are you thinking about?"

"I'm thinking about you," I said. "You are a man in the prime of life, a distinguished man, a clever man, but a lonely man. What you need is a wife, a wife who is worthy of you, a young and charming and also efficient wife. She should be a woman who would do everything for her husband. Not only would she cook for him and cater to his every taste, but she would also be his constant comfort. When he is downcast, she would make him happy; when he is happy, she would make him happier. In the morning she would brighten the day with a delicious breakfast, and she would make the evening cozy when she

brought him his pipe and slippers. When he wanted to relax, she would entertain him with the latest gossip; when he wanted to work, she would see that he was not disturbed. She——"

"She! She! She!" cried Mirvin. "Where is this wonderful she? And where are the thousand gold coins?"

"They are not far away," I answered. "The two things can be brought together. I happen to know where the girl can be found. And the gold has not been touched."

"It is a most unlikely story," grumbled Mirvin. "It sounds like a fairy tale you made up. Still, I might believe it if I could have a look at the gold and the girl—the gold first."

"I can take you to the place where the gold is hidden," I said. "But you must promise not to take any part of the treasure. As I said, all of it must remain where it is until the right time."

"Who said anything about taking?" said Mirvin. "I just want to see whether you are telling the truth."

"Very well," I said. "You will see. We will leave the house after it grows dark. Take a lantern with you, for the treasure is at the bottom of a well."

Mirvin did as he was told. I led him to the deserted house of my dead mistress. We climbed over crumbling walls and stumbled across paths overgrown with briars. Finally we reached the well. Mirvin lifted the lantern and peered down. Something glittered in the depths.

"I see them!" cried Mirvin in great excitement. "Are you sure there are a thousand?"

"I never counted them," I said. "I know only what she told me— and you can see for yourself."

"I'll take your word for it now that I have some evidence," said Mirvin. "Here, as you say, is the treasure, and here"—he pointed to himself—"is the man. Now, where is the girl?"

"Have a little patience," I said. "First things first. First let me ask you a question. Are you sure you want so much money? Money is always a great problem as well as a great temptation. It tempts you to own all sorts of things. As soon as you get all that money you will buy fine clothes and expensive furniture to impress the neighbors. You will enlarge your property. You will build barns; you will have cows and horses and servants to take care of them. You will have many things to worry about, many things to remember—what to tell the gardener to plant, what sort of clothes to wear for everyday and what sort for holidays, what kind of wine to serve with what kind of food, what investments to make at what time of the year, what kind of people to cultivate, what——"

"Stop your chattering!" interrupted Mirvin. "Fetch me the money. I'll know what to do with it. As for the girl, I ask you again, where is she?"

"Don't worry," I said. "I know just where she can be reached."

"Good," said Mirvin. "I will give you three more days to produce her. No longer. Now you can go."

In my wanderings over the rooftops I had met an owl, a most remarkable bird. He lived in the chimney of a house that belonged to an old woman who, like Mirvin, was a worker in magic. Unlike Mirvin, she was a simple, goodhearted person. She loved children, was pleasant to people, and disliked no one—no one except Mirvin. She believed that he had evil thoughts as well as evil powers. She enjoyed being a witch, partly for the fun of it, and partly because she helped people with her harmless witchcraft. She made powders to prevent fevers, pills to ease pain, and potions to bring parted lovers together. Everything she made was lovingly prepared with sweet-smelling flowers and spicy herbs: roses and rosemary, carnations

and clove, milkweed and mace, syringa and sage. All week long she washed and cooked, cleaned house, and puttered around her garden like any other old woman. But on weekends she became an entirely different person. Then, with the aid of a secret formula, her wrinkles disappeared, her shabby clothes dropped off, and the rather ugly old woman turned herself into a lovely young girl. Mounting a broomstick, she would rise through the chimney and soar naked through the air. Galloping on her one-footed horse, she would laugh and sing, her lips shining like polished cherries and her long yellow hair flying like a flag in the wind.

The owl was her servant. From his perch in the chimney he advised her about the weather; he knew when the clouds gathered and when the wind was good or bad for flying. It was to the owl that I went with a plan.

"Good evening, Master Owl," I said. "I see you are still keeping watch. To relieve your boredom I thought you might like a little conversation. Before we talk, here is a mouse I picked up on my way. It isn't much, but I hope you'll accept it."

"Thanks," said the owl. "It's a fine mouse. In return do me the favor of accepting this small sparrow that happened to fly too close."

For a short while the two of us sat chewing and crunching. Then the owl spoke again.

"You haven't given your friends the pleasure of your company in some time. What has been happening to you?"

I told him everything—how Mirvin and I had made a bargain, how I had been fed and overfed, how I had almost been killed, and how I had managed to save myself.

"You talked yourself out of a dangerous situation," said the owl. "Now you are free to go anywhere and do anything."

"Not quite," I said. "First I must do something about the treasure.

And then I must get that girl for Mirvin."

"What!" exclaimed the owl. "Are you mad? You certainly are not going to reward the man who tried to cut away your fat and take the skin off your back!"

"It won't be exactly a reward," I said. "I want to pay Mirvin back for what he tried to do to me, pay him back in, let's say, his own coin."

"What *about* those coins?" asked owl. "Are they real, and are there a thousand of them?"

"They are real enough," I said. "But there are only a few of them, a dozen or so. A robber had hidden them in the old lady's well, expecting to come back for them. But he was killed by another robber, and my mistress would never touch the coins. 'It is stolen money,' she said, 'and it has caused death. There is a curse on it, and it will bring bad luck to anyone who touches it.'"

"You are a clever one," said the owl. "But what about the girl? Where is she to come from?"

"From this chimney," I said. "Wouldn't you like your freedom? Wouldn't it be wonderful if we got Mirvin, the wicked wizard, married to your mistress, the old witch?"

"It would be wonderful indeed," said the owl. "But how do you propose to bring this about?"

"First," I said, "we must catch our witch."

"How is that to be done?" inquired the owl.

"With a net," I replied. "With the very same net Mirvin uses to catch his croaking blackbirds. It is a tightly woven net made from the toughest hemp. Nothing can break through it. It is lying in the corner of Mirvin's kitchen. Fetch it, and we shall put it to better use than snaring troublemaking birds."

The owl flew off and was back in a few minutes, carrying the net in his beak. Together we stretched it over the chimney and waited. It was a weekend, and we did not have a long time to wait.

When the church clock struck the hour of midnight we heard a rustle from below. At the twelfth stroke a voice called out.

"What is the weather like up there?"

"Fine and foul," replied the owl. "Fine and foul. An ideal night for flying."

A moment later something white came up the chimney. There was a scream—and our witch lay tangled in the net. She raged and kicked and cried. She tried to tear herself loose. But the net held, and after a while she tired of squirming in the trap. Finally she spoke.

"A witch bewitched! By a cat and an owl! It's too absurd! I should be outraged, but"—here she gave a little laugh—"I am amused. Why did you two odd creatures do it?"

"I wanted my liberty," said the owl.

"That's easily granted," said the witch. "You could have had it anytime. All you had to do was ask for it. And what does your strange companion want?"

"I want you to marry Mirvin the magician," I said.

"Marry that hateful man? Not I. Never! I'll spend the rest of my life in this net rather than live with that selfish, stupid, scoundrelly, good-for-nothing fraud!"

"You wouldn't want the whole town to see you hanging from the chimney, would you?" I said. "Of course not. As for Mirvin, think a minute. Think how much pleasure it would give you to master him, to make him fetch and carry, to train him to do your bidding and make him the laughingstock of the town."

There was a pause. It was broken by a chuckle.

"There is something in what you propose," she said. "Mirvin should certainly be taught a lesson. You seem to have a plan, and you obviously expect me to help you. What do you have in mind?"

I told her about my bargain with Mirvin, told her exactly what she could do: how she was to find the well, bring up the coins, arrange them, and the next morning, go to the town gate. Then I went back to Mirvin.

"The gold has been recovered and the girl has been found," I told him. "I have explained everything to her. She will be at the town gate, all alone, tomorrow morning."

The next day Mirvin was up at dawn. He dressed himself carefully, putting on his holiday clothes, a handsome vest, velvet coat, silk hose, and gay green gloves. He put a flower in his buttonhole and sprinkled himself with a love potion. Sticking a perfumed handkerchief in his pocket, he swaggered down the street.

When he came to the town gate, there she was, young and lovely and shy.

"They told me about you," she said. "I have been lonely waiting."

"You need wait no longer," said Mirvin. "Nor will you be lonely. Will you marry me?"

"A girl should ask for time before she answers such a question," she murmured. "She should not seem too eager. But"—she smiled—"they tell me that she who hesitates is lost. So I will not hesitate. The answer is yes."

Mirvin hurried her off to an old hermit who lived at the edge of the town, and the hermit pronounced them husband and wife. Then Mirvin took her to his house, where he had prepared a wedding breakfast. There were no other guests except the owl and myself.

It was quite an occasion. Mirvin proposed several toasts, the owl and I sang several duets, and throughout it all the bride sat smiling. Mirvin's eyes were on her every moment, except when they were looking greedily at the gold coins she had brought and put in a bowl on the table. He particularly admired her piled-up yellow hair, which seemed to him like a pile of glittering gold pieces.

"This is no time to complain," said Mirvin, pointing to the coins. "There aren't as many as promised, not nearly as many. Still, I know how to invest them so that there will be many, many more."

He ran a few of the coins lovingly through his fingers, and as he dropped them back in the bowl, a peculiar thing happened. The gold coins changed into yellow kernels, kernels of common corn.

Mirvin was horribly shocked. He struck his forehead. "Who is playing tricks?" he shouted. His agonized outcry was followed by another sound, a softer yet stranger sound. His bride was laughing.

More startled than ever, Mirvin looked at her. And as he looked, she too changed. Her piled-up yellow hair fell down in a tangled gray mass; the cupid's-bow of her lips straightened into a thin line; her bright blue eyes turned dull brown; and her smooth ivory brow was a network of ugly wrinkles.

Mirvin gasped. He refused to believe what he saw, refused to believe he had married a witch, and an ugly old witch at that.

She continued to laugh, shrilly now, and her voice was so loud that people in the street could hear her.

"O master magician," she laughed scornfully, "your greed has brought about your own punishment, and your black magic has done you no good. Next time you will think twice before you do something wicked. Next time you won't be in such a hurry to buy the fat off a poor cat."

People heard and laughed at that last remark. They began to repeat it. Soon it became a proverb. Even today in Switzerland, when someone tries to drive a hard bargain, they say, "Don't be in a hurry to buy the fat off the cat."

I was, of course, delighted with the way things had turned out. Mirvin fussed and fumed, but it did him no good. The witch paid no

attention to him. She grew very fond of me, fed me from the table, and had me sleep at the foot of her bed. During the day she kept me at her side, and night after night I rode with her on the broomstick. We sailed over the rooftops, into the clouds, over the town, and into the country. It was a wonderful life. Once more I had everything a cat could want, more than I had ever hoped to have. I grew soft and round; my fur shone. I was myself, Silky, again.

THE EIGHTH LIFE
HOW I MADE A POOR BOY RICH

Except for a single foreign adventure, my eighth life was spent entirely in London. I was a London cat from the top of my nose to the tip of my tail. I knew every street, lane, and alley from Cheapside to Chelsea, from the cluttered docks along the Thames to the elegant mansions of Berkeley Square, from the Billingsgate fish market to the fashion center of Bond Street. I lived by my wits. Sometimes my stomach was comfortably full; sometimes it was painfully empty. Sometimes I had my pick of good things in back of fancy restaurants; sometimes I had to fight other hungry cats for what some dog had left; sometimes I hunted for horrid remnants floating in the gutters. But I enjoyed every moment of my vagabond life and every inch of the great city.

No beauty, I was nobody's pet. I asked no favors of anyone. A loner, I liked nothing better than being on my own. People did not interest me; I went out of my way to avoid them.

One evening, however, something happened that made me feel different about human beings. I noticed a boy walking slowly along the pavement. There was nothing new about boys running around the streets; I had passed hundreds of them without a thought. But there was something about this boy—something in the way he walked and kept on turning his head made me curious. For one thing, he was not a Londoner. His clothes, his hesitating steps, his uncertainty about which corner to turn told me he was from the country. He was thin; he looked hungry. He would stop strangers and ask questions that I could not hear. He did not seem to be begging, but the people he spoke to shook their heads.

As I said, I was curious—I have always had an inquisitive nature—so I followed him. I saw that he was weary; he stumbled several times, and once he fell. And then, in front of a bakery, inhaling the warm smell of fresh rolls, he fainted. When he got up, his face was white; he trembled and his hands shook. His legs could not take him much farther. He collapsed in the doorway of a large house, his head propped against a wall.

It was dark now, dark and cold. I drew close to him. Then I did something I had never done before. I don't know why I did it, but I crept into the boy's lap. He put his arms around me and pulled me to his chest. "Kitty, kitty," he murmured, and fell asleep.

The next thing I remember was a door banging and a woman's voice as loud as the bang.

"What impudence! To use Mr. Fitzwarren's front doorway for your sleeping quarters! You and your cat!" She shook the boy roughly. "Out! Get out!"

The boy began to weep, and I set up a wail. With the woman's

scolding, the boy's weeping, and my wailing, we made a considerable noise. Then I heard another voice, a man's voice.

"What is this, Mrs. Bean? Why all the commotion?"

"Beg pardon, Mr. Fitzwarren," said the woman. "But it's hard enough keeping the entrance clean these days of drought and dust. To make it harder, the wind has blown in a dirty boy and his very common cat."

"Mrs. Bean, the boy looks ill, and it's plain he's half starved. Take him to the kitchen and tell cook to give him a hot breakfast. As for his cat, I think we could spare the creature a saucer of milk. Afterward I would like a word with the boy."

An hour later Mrs. Bean took us to Mr. Fitzwarren's study. It was a large room lined with books and engraved portraits. Mr. Fitzwarren sat at a long table that held charts and models of merchant ships. The boy stood on the threshold, too timid to advance.

"Come in, my lad," said Mr. Fitzwarren. "What's your name?"

"Dick," whispered the boy.

"Dick who?"

"Dick Whittington, sir."

"There's no reason to be frightened. Speak up. Where are you from and what brought you here?"

The boy leaned over and patted me. It seemed to reassure him.

"My home was in Sussex. I was a few years old when my parents died, and an uncle took charge of me. When he died I was all alone. I helped a farmer during the haying season, but when it was over he said he had no room for a boy who was still growing and always hungry."

"Then what did you do?" asked Mr. Fitzwarren.

"I made up my mind to come to London. I had heard that the streets were paved with gold and that everyone in London was rich.

I didn't really believe it, but I thought it would be easy to find work here."

"How did you get here? London is a long way from Sussex."

"A carter gave me a life to Guildford, and another driver brought me to the markets at Covent Garden. But I could find no work there or anywhere. Times were hard, they told me, and no one was being hired."

"Well, Dick," said Mr. Fitzwarren, "I think we can find something for you. There's plenty to do around the house, especially in the kitchen. Suppose you start there. Try not to get under the cook's heels and try not to mind Mrs. Bean's tongue."

"Thank you," said the boy. "May I keep the cat?"

"I would not separate sleeping companions," said Mr. Fitzwarren, smiling. "I don't think cook will mind. Your cat might get rid of the mice that she says are always making their home in the pantry. Besides, it may amuse my daughter Alice, who is about your age. What do you call your cat?"

"He hasn't had a name yet," said the boy. "But he is so soft and fluffy that I'm going to call him Fluff."

This was an unbelievable exaggeration. I was a somewhat scrawny short-haired cat; nothing could have been less fluffy. But I was touched by the boy's illusions, and I was happy to answer to the name of Fluff.

Months went by, and for about a year things went well. The work was not too hard; we were well fed; there was plenty of time to play. I was petted by Alice almost as fondly as I was by the boy, a boy who was rapidly becoming a young man.

Then Mr. Fitzwarren went abroad and everything changed. The cook was not easy to get along with; she could not tolerate anyone else in her kitchen and she disliked cats. But it was Mrs. Bean, the housekeeper, who made our lives almost impossible. She made Dick do the work of half a dozen men. Day after day he had to clean all the cutlery, polish dozens of pewter dishes, scrub the pots and pans, scour countless platters, sweep the steps, clear away the ashes in the fireplace, dust the furniture, beat the rugs, wash and wipe cartloads of dishes, and run numberless errands. She also hurt him by mistreating me. She mocked him cruelly when he protected me, and when he complained, she made him work still harder. Alice sympathized, but she could do nothing to help

Things got so bad that Dick's only hope was the return of Mr. Fitzwarren, but he could not find out when the master was coming back, if at all. He decided to run away.

"We can't go on like this, Fluff," he said. "We're quitting this place and going back to Sussex. I'm older now and I'm sure to find work in the country."

Something told me not to leave London, but I was Dick Whittington's cat, and I knew he loved me and needed me. I went with him. When we reached the outskirts of the city he paused, uncertain how to go on. I pulled at his trousers and mewed, trying to tell him to turn back. At that very moment church bells began to ring. They sounded the same chime over and over. Dick sprang to his feet.

"Listen, Fluff!" he cried in great excitement. "Do you hear what the bells are ringing? They are not going *ding-dong, ding-dong*. They are *saying* something, something meant for me. They are saying, *'Dick, Dick, turn again, Dick Whittington. One, two, three—you will be—three times Lord Mayor of London.'* Of course that's ridiculous. But that's what the bells keep on saying. Foolish it may be, but I'm going to heed those bells. Come on, Fluff, we're going back."

I knew I had been right in not wishing to leave London. When we returned no one noticed us. There was much running to and fro, for

the house was being made ready for the return of Mr. Fitzwarren. The next morning he arrived. With him was the captain of one of his merchant ships.

Toward afternoon Dick was called to Mr. Fitzwarren's study. I was at his heels. The captain was seated at the table.

"Dick," said Mr. Fitzwarren, "one of my ships is sailing tomorrow to trade in North Africa. Besides the usual cargo, there will be domestic goods to be sold. I have always allowed members of my household to have some share in the proceeds. Most of the servants have contributed one thing or another for sale. Is there anything you would like to sell?"

"I have nothing," said Dick. "Nothing except Fluff, and I wouldn't sell him for the world."

"Well spoken," said the captain. "I would not offer to buy your pet. But, my boy, I would be glad to rent him. My ship is overrun with pests, and your cat looks like an excellent mouser and ratter. It won't be too long a trip, and I will pay you ten shillings for the loan of your Fluff. What do you say?"

Dick looked at me. Then he looked at Mr. Fitzwarren, and Mr. Fitzwarren nodded his head.

"I think you should do it," he said. "It would be a real experience for the cat, and the ten shillings may be a kind of nest egg for your future earnings."

That is how I had my foreign adventure. I was not happy to be separated from my young master, but I must admit I enjoyed the voyage. The food was coarse, but it was different (I've always liked novelty) and there was plenty of it. Hunting was a continual pleasure; it didn't take me long to rid the ship of rats. The sailors made much of me. Even the first mate, who said he had never been able to abide a cat, liked to pick me up and play with me. Everyone laughed when

I jumped up on an empty chair at the captain's table. "Let him stay," said the captain. "I don't know how we ever got along without Fluff."

We stopped at many ports, trading and trafficking. While the men went ashore to buy and sell, the first mate and I remained on the ship. One evening in Morocco the captain came back with an odd smile on his face.

"This is a queer place," he said to the first mate. "I wouldn't have believed it if I hadn't seen it with my own eyes."

"What happened?" asked the first mate.

"When I showed our merchandise to the chief trader this morning," said the captain, "he told me that the ruler of the country was greatly interested in such wares. He took me to the palace, and we arrived there just as the midday meal was being served. All sorts of silver platters were brought in with much ceremony. But as soon as the covers were removed a horde of mice and rats swarmed over the food. They snapped up all the dainty morsels and carried off the larger pieces. There was little left for the diners. 'This is horrible!' I said to the ruler. 'Why do you permit it?'

"'It is something we cannot help,' replied the ruler. 'The cook has to prepare three times the amount of food so that something is left for us. We have tried to clear the palace of the greedy vermin, but without success. Even when they are glutted, they attack us while we sleep. I cannot tell you how much I would give anyone who knew a way to get rid of them.'

"I told him that I knew a way and that I would show it to him the next day."

"You mean Fluff," said the first mate.

"Of course," said the captain. "There wasn't a sign of a cat any-where, and I realized that he had never even heard of one."

The following day toward noon the captain put me in a covered basket and carried me to the palace. When the meal was served he placed the basket next to him. As soon as the dishes were uncovered and the rodents appeared he let me out. I did not have to be told what to do. I went to work and in less than an hour more than thirty mice and a dozen rats lay dead. I scorned to eat them; far more tempting fare was waiting for me. After I had washed my paws and cleaned my whiskers, the ruler said, "What a marvelous creature! I must have it. Name your price."

"I am sorry," said the captain, "but he is not for sale."

"I will give you anything. I will give you his weight in gold."

"Impossible," said the captain. "He does not belong to me. But I will do this. I will lend him to you for a month. There is trading to be done in other ports. On our return voyage next month I will pick him up, and then you can pay me whatever his services were worth."

The ruler was delighted, and so was I. I was treated not only with respect but with awe. I was pampered to the limit. I was considered too precious to pick up and pet, but I was lovingly handled. A gem-studded collar was tied around my neck, and the richest food was always on my plate. When I was in danger of giving myself airs, I had to remind myself that I was really nothing but a London alley cat, a cat who was here on business. And the business went well. When the ship returned, there was not a mouse or a rat anywhere in the neighborhood.

"He has earned our thanks as well as our love," said the ruler to the captain. "Here is something to show our appreciation. My servants will carry it to your ship."

It was a beautiful box of aromatic wood tied with many-colored bands, and it stayed sealed until it was taken to Mr. Fitzwarren.

After the business arrangements had been settled, the captain brought me in with the box and asked for Dick.

"Here is the cat I borrowed," he said when Dick entered. "But you gave him the wrong name. Instead of Fluff, you should have called him Rough or Tough. You should have seen what he did in that Moroccan palace! Here are the ten shillings. And"—he told all that had happened—"here is an extra return for the loan."

The captain opened the box, and drew out of it a mass of silks, embroidered tapestries, gold coins, and precious gems.

Dick stared and could scarcely speak. Then, shaking his head, he said, "No. Such a treasure is not for me. It should go to Mr. Fitzwarren. Besides, I have Fluff again, and that is enough."

"You deserve it, my lad," said Mr. Fitzwarren. "You owe it to Fluff, and to yourself too. If you wish, I will take care of it and see that you get the best return for it."

Mr. Fitzwarren did just that. He sold the jewels, changed the gold coins into English money, and invested the proceeds in merchandise to be shipped and traded abroad. Later he and Dick became partners, and when he died, Dick, still in his twenties, became a wealthy man. He married Alice, who had been in love with him ever since she first saw him. The bells had predicted truly. He became Lord Mayor of London not just once but three times.

When he was knighted by the king, my master, now Sir Richard Whittington, moved into a grand mansion.

"Both of us will have to get accustomed to living in style, Fluff," he said to me. "To show that it is your home as well as mine, I will have a sculpture of you placed over the front door. It will tell the world I owe everything to a cat, a cat who made a poor boy rich."

I was, of course, pleased. But what pleased me most was what the sculpture accomplished. The carving was so lifelike that not a single mouse dared to cross the threshold.

THE NINTH LIFE
HOW I
CAME TO LIFE
FOR AN HOUR

My ninth life was the shortest of all my lives. It was also the strangest. It began as a thought in the mind of a small boy. This was Toshio, a Japanese boy, the youngest of a very poor family.

He was no different from other boys and girls who lived in Kyoto except in one way: he was mad about cats. There was neither room nor food enough in his shabby little house for a pet, but cats collected around the door, and he kept scraps from his own food to feed them. Cats followed him when he walked down the street; he talked to every cat he met, and he believed that cats talked to him. He dreamed of nothing but cats. Before he learned to write, he drew pictures of cats, cats of every kind and color, portraits of cats that he knew and of cats that never existed. He was not very good at it, but that was all he wanted to do.

His father thought this was a childish weakness and that the boy would get over it. He hoped Toshio would become a priest and took him to the temple at Nara. The bonze, a Buddhist monk, met them and led them through the beautifully curved torii that was the gateway into the dusky interior to the great statue of Buddha.

"It is my hope that my son will serve in this temple," said Toshio's father. "I hope you will teach him the things he should know. He is a good boy and should make a good priest."

"He is very young," said the bonze. "But not too young to be of help in the temple. If he obeys the rules, he might become an attendant in a little time. It is a beginning."

So Toshio began. But he was not a good scholar. When he should have been studying, he was thinking about cats. When he took up his writing box to copy the lessons, he did not write. He drew cats.

The old bonze shook his head. "Toshio," he said, "you are a good boy and someday you may be a good artist. But you will never be a priest. It would be best for you to try something else. Meanwhile, go home."

Toshio was ashamed. He knew that his father would be disappointed and that his brothers and sisters would make fun of him. He did not know what to do or where to go. But he knew he did not want to go home. He walked out of the temple, out of the town, not sure where his feet were taking him.

He walked, it seemed, for hours. As it got dark he grew weary and looked for somewhere to sleep. Ahead of him was a temple, smaller than the one he had left in Nara, but one that seemed to offer shelter. When he approached it, he saw that the main doors were boarded up and that there was a sign saying "Do not enter." Then he remembered a story the bonze had told about a deserted temple that had been taken over by a monster. No one could describe the monster for no one had seen it. Several priests armed with swords had gone to the temple to get rid of the thing, whatever it was, but they had disappeared, and their bodies had never been found.

Toshio was too weary to go farther. "Besides," he said to himself, "it's only a story; there are no monsters anymore." He found a side door that was ajar and slipped in. He was about to settle himself in a corner when he noticed the screens. There were many of them, large white screens made of paper, and there were no designs on them. Tired as he was, it was too tempting. He began to draw.

He drew cats of every size, kind, and color, in every possible position, cats alone and cats in company, cats curled up on the floor and cats springing through the air, cats feeding quietly and cats arching their backs with the threat of war, cats yawning with the surfeit of a full stomach and cats fighting furiously. He was not satisfied with any of them. The drawings were fairly good but they were not real enough. He was terribly tired, but he could not stop drawing. He determined to make one more sketch before he fell asleep.

This time he worked slowly and far more carefully. He used his brush judiciously, adding a line here, a line there, paying the strictest attention to the swelling of a curve, the thin sweep of a whisker, the needle point of a claw. Little by little the drawing became something more than a drawing. It had vitality; it quivered. The eyes glowed, the hair glistened, blood began to flow through its veins. The drawing was coming to life. It was a true creation, the Complete Cat. It was I!

Satisfied with what he had done, Toshio had fallen asleep. But I was awake. I was alive—alive and alert—ready for anything. But I was still motionless on the screen. I wanted desperately to stretch. I thought, "If only I could flex my muscles, move about, and feel the thrill of action. If only I could have a chance for excitement! If I had only one hour of life!"

Then, in a darkness so great that you could feel the weight of

blackness, I heard something stir. It began with a hissing sound that grew into a howl and filled the temple with horror. I will never know how it happened, but at that moment I was released. I sprang from the screen and leaped at the unseen thing. I used everything I had—teeth, claws, striking power, even my tail—until the thing lay still and the temple was empty of sound.

In the morning I was once more motionless, on the screen as before. There was an indescribable mess, the remains of some kind of horrible corpse, on the floor of the temple. Toshio woke and stared at it. Then he stared at me and ran to the door. He called, and some people hurried in.

"Look at what's on the floor!" cried Toshio. "And look at that cat! I drew it last night. It is only a drawing, but see! There is blood, real blood, dripping from its jaws!"

I had had my hour of life.

ONE MORE WORD

After I told the last story, someone said I was a storyteller in every sense. I suppose that meant I was not always telling the truth. The truth is that some of the things that happened to me have been borrowed by others. The tale about Dick Whittington and his cat is now part of English folklore; but it was I who lived with the boy and made him famous before anything was written about him. The same is true of the Puss-in-Boots story. It too has become a legend; but I was the puss that did the trick and saw my firsthand account turned into a fairy tale. You will find a feeble and completely false account of my life as a human being in Aesop's *Fables.* A Swiss writer by the name of Gottfried Keller made a long-winded version of the way I outwitted a magician in "Spiegel das Kätzchen." An American author, Lafcadio Hearn, took an idea of mine and made up "The Boy Who Drew Cats."

So far no one has rewritten my accounts of how I led an army, how I made friends with mice, how I saved my country, how I lived as a human being, and how I became a god. But I am sure that someday someone will.

Everyone has a right not only to tell stories but also to retell them. Even though it's true that I helped to make some authors famous, I don't boast about it. And I don't complain. There is fame enough for all of us.